To All the Girls I've Loved Before: Sexy Short Stories Book 3

Dirk Caldwell Sexy Short Stories, Volume 3

Dirk Caldwell

Published by Dirk Caldwell, 2024.

TO ALL THE GIRLS I'VE LOVED BEFORE: SEXY SHORT STORIES BOOK 3

First edition. October 29, 2024.

Copyright © 2024 Dirk Caldwell.

ISBN: 979-8227757791

Written by Dirk Caldwell.

Also by Dirk Caldwell

Adventures of Stan
Stan does a Big Girl and gives her a Big Orgasm
Stan Does a Female Police Officer While On Duty
Stan Scores on a Booty Call with Barbara
Stan Takes Barb's Anal Cherry
Stan Teaches Oklahoma Karen About Sex in the City
Stan gets Kinky with Barb on Vacation
Barb Wants more Orgasms with Stan before She gets Engaged to Another Man
Stan Does Barbara's Mom!
Stan Titty Fucks Barbara's Friend!

Dirk Caldwell Romantic Erotic Novels
A Visit to the Farm with Darla - a Sexy Short Story
A Layover in Omaha with Tina
A Night in Eufaula with Lynn
A Trip to the Lake with Kim
Older Women need Love, too! Erika visits Atlanta
Lessons in Love: Gabriella visits Indianapolis
Big Girls Need Love, too! Barbara from Kokomo
Flight Attendants want Love: Flying High with Jessica
Back to the Farm with Darla - A Sexy Sequel

Redheads need Love: Megan from New Orleans
A Big Girl finds Love: Joann from Shreveport
Lust from London: My Affair with a British Nymphomaniac
Paula's Sexy European Weekend
Mother and Daughter Threesome

Dirk Caldwell Sexy Short Stories
To All the Girls I've Loved Before: Sexy Short Stories Book 1
To All the Girls I've Loved Before: Sexy Short Stories Book 2
To All the Girls I've Loved Before: Sexy Short Stories Book 3

Table of Contents

Acknowledgment

AI Cover image by Freepik

Introduction

I was giving Jackie a titty fuck in the shower as she knelt before me and held my rock hard cock between her big boobs. Earlier, she had blown me as I sat on the edge of the hotel bed, then I fucked her and took her to breakfast. Back at her place, I gave her a first orgasm by going down on her, and she'd taken my load of cum in her mouth as my reward. She'd promised to let me fuck her in the ass later, but I had an urgent need to ejaculate on her tits. I'll explain how I came to be in the position with Jackie and three other fantastic women.

My name is Dirk. Well, that's not my real name. I'd never be able to have a normal life if I used my real name. I was an enlisted guy in the Air Force and single at the time of this encounter. I enjoyed being unencumbered and the benefits that came from that. I could travel the world as an international military aircrew member and be with any woman I wanted without regret and have always enjoyed the freedom that came with that ability.

I enjoy recalling some of my favorite encounters. Most were great, some were just okay, and some I absolutely could not believe what happened. These are the encounters I write about, as they are the most entertaining and fun to read about. While most of the content in my stories is true, I do spice things up now and then, but you would be surprised how much happened exactly as written. I've been incredibly lucky with women and am humbled every day that I have had so much success.

As a disclaimer, I always change enough of the information about the ladies so my writing could not possibly be traced back to them. Most cities are changed, along with names, occupations, specific characteristics, branches of service for the military, etc. To do otherwise would not be gentlemanly. I do, however, mix in some of my local knowledge about locations. How did I get that information? Let your imagination be your guide.

I hope you enjoy this novel. Please check out more of my works at the same place you purchased this one.

Louise

I had undressed the drunken mid-40s aged woman that I had talked into coming to my hotel room. She was laying naked on my bed looking up at me impassively with glassy eyes as I fondled her middle-aged body that was twice my age. Then I reached for her pussy. Attempting to put my finger in her to stimulate her, I ran into something I had not yet encountered in my brief sexual experience. Her vagina was as dry as a stick. There was no way I was getting my stiff cock in there. What do I do now?

This encounter describes one of my earliest sexual adventures. I was 21 years old, and an Air Force airplane mechanic stationed in California. I was assigned to another base for a few days of temporary duty with several colleagues from my shop. Here is the story.

My trip was a short one. Some of my colleagues and I drove from our base near Sacramento, California to a base further south in the San Joaquin valley, near Merced, CA. We made short work of our first day of duty and all had skipped dinner so we could start drinking at a country and western themed bar adjacent to our hotel.

We were all pretty lit by the middle of the evening when the band started, and for some reason I wanted to corral one of the many unaccompanied women that filled the place and take one to my room and fuck her. This was probably due to my 21-year-old raging testosterone and an urge to show how cool I was to my friends. I was dancing with and putting the make on every female that would talk to me. Several mixed drinks had lowered my inhibitions.

After a while I had focused my attention on a semi-attractive woman in her 40s who was paying attention to me as I sweet talked her. She was drunk, and I thought my chances were good to get between her legs. We engaged in some small talk as we danced.

"I'm Louise."

"Dirk."

"I haven't seen you in here before, Dirk."

"It's my first time. I'm here in town for a few days for the Air Force."

She smiled as we swayed together with our arms around each other.

"I see. Where are you staying, out at the air base?"

"No, at the Holiday Inn next door."

"I think you like me a little. You've danced with me three times now."

"Of course I like you, Lousie. You're a nice-looking lady and are a lot of fun."

She grinned.

"That's not what I meant."

She kept eye contact with me as she pushed her hips into my erection. Oops.

"Sorry, Louise."

"Don't be sorry, sugar. I take it as a compliment."

To emphasize her point, she pushed her hips into my erection again, still looking into my eyes and still smiling. This showed potential and gave us more to talk about as she ran her hands over my arms and up and down my back.

"Young men like you are usually in nice shape and have good stamina in bed. So much better than men my age."

"I suppose that's true. I like to think that I have good stamina."

Louise was making it clear that she liked to fuck young guys. My ears had perked up. After another minute of dancing, I decided to be bold.

"I like it when you push into me with your hips."

She smiled again and gave me another shove with her hips, giving me a little grind against my boner.
"Like that?"

"Oh, yeah. That feels good."
She nodded wisely.
"Well, you're really gonna like this!"

With that, she reached between us and gave my bulging cock a squeeze with her hand, right there on the dance floor. Not exactly subtle.
"You're right. I like that a lot. But I hate to think you're just teasing me."
She shook her head as she gave it another squeeze.
"No, I'm not teasing. Let's call it warming up. After this dance, let's go to your hotel."
I tried to sound casual, like it was no big deal.
"Sure, that would be nice."
As the dance ended, she held my hand as I led her back to her table of friends. She leaned over to me and whispered.
"Let me say goodbye to my friends, then meet me at the door."
After gulping down my drink when I got back to my table, I said good night to my colleagues, including my Master Sergeant, who was quite pleased with me.
"Give it a shove for me, kid!" He called out as I headed for the door.

I was fairly pleased with myself. I had successfully cut Louise out from the herd, and with my colleagues watching and giving me a thumbs up, I walked out of the bar accompanied by her with a gleam in my eye and hope for getting some pussy in my heart.

Louise led me to her car, a late model Cadillac, red in color. At the driver door, I put my arms around her and kissed her, to keep her in the mood for sex, which I'm sure she was thinking about. She responded hungrily, and after a while we got in her car, with me giving her directions to go to the motel just next door. A problem was she was so drunk it was difficult to get to the hotel without the Cadillac colliding with stationary objects. We finally made it to the hotel unscathed, and I got her to my room without being seen by anyone.

Once in the room, she dropped her huge purse on the bed and turned toward me with a grin. We kissed again, and I started fondling her outside of her clothing, then we sat on the bed and continued. With youthful vigor, I was undressing her as I went, with no protests noted from Louise.

Soon I had her blouse and bra off and was playing with her big boobs and nipples as she watched me with interest. After a while, she started to take my shirt off, and caressed my chest. Then she lay back on the bed smiling up at me. I took the opportunity to remove her shoes, knee high stockings, slacks, and underwear. Within a short period of time, she was naked.

I had never seen a middle-aged woman naked before, so I took in the sights. Her hair was medium length and dyed black, coifed in a mature style. She wore heavy makeup with blue eyeshadow and had dark red lipstick. There were some lines on her face, which was starting to get fleshy. Her neck had some extra flesh, and as I said, her boobs were nice and big while a bit saggy, the nipples pink and pert. The stomach had some extra flesh, with a roll around her waist. The thighs and legs were nothing special, just normal woman legs. She had a medium dark-haired bush of hair at her crotch, which I was looking at intently as my finger was attempting to enter the vagina.

As I pondered what to do about the dry love canal, Louise spoke for the first time since we had arrived in the room.

"Get some lotion out of the bathroom. They always have those little bottles."

I jumped up and found a little pink bottle of the stuff and brought it to her. She opened the bottle and reached between her legs and applied the stuff as I watched in fascination. She applied it to her labia and smiling at me, put some on a finger and worked it into the vaginal vault. It was pretty erotic watching a woman finger herself, getting lubed up for sex. Lou then reached for my hand and poured some of the lotion on my fingers.

"Now you do it."

She watched as I reached my lotion covered fingers to her labia and inserted one.

"Mmm. Use two fingers."

I did, and she closed her eyes and smiled for a moment as I applied the lotion. Things were nice and slippery now.

"That's good. Come here."

Louise reached for my stiff cock and applied some lotion to it, coating the head and stroking some down the shaft. She looked at me and smiled.

"Your dick is hard as a board! Good. I like young, hard cocks. Let's see how you do."

She tossed the lotion aside and held her arms out for me. I knelt between her legs and moved up to put my cock up to her hairy pussy. She pulled on my cock, lining it up, then looked at me with a drunken grin.

"Well, go ahead! You've been wanting that all night, so have at it!"

Encouraged, I pushed into her gently, then fully. She closed her eyes and smiled again. I guess I was doing something right. My cock was all the way in, and I started a gentle thrusting, rapidly increasing the pace. She opened her eyes after a minute of intense stroking.

"Slow down, sugar! It's not a race!"

I slowed down, very much feeling like the rookie that I was. My sexual experience thus far was with women my age. Well, there was that one woman that was eight years older, but that's another story. This was my first experience with a woman that probably a generation older. Her lubricated pussy felt nice, and the boobs jiggled nicely as I thrust into her, but there was a lot of differences to absorb. She spoke again.

"I can tell you're about to come. Don't blow your wad inside me, pull out and put your cock on my belly. Better do it now, I bet you're about to pop!"

I pulled my slimy dick out and moved forward, laying it on her fleshy stomach. She reached for my dick and started jacking me off, and within seconds I ejaculated onto her belly, shooting spurt upon spurt of sticky cum, filling up her belly button and making a mess. Total elapsed time of copulation was about a minute and a half. While it felt good to come, I was feeling embarrassed at my hair triggered cock.

Louise laughed and commented with slurred speech.

"That's okay, baby. We needed to get that first one over with. You'll last longer for the next one. Go on to the bathroom and get me a warm, wet washcloth. You can clean up the mess you made."

I soon had her wiped down and joined her back on the bed.

"Come on and lay next to me. You can play with my boobs and pussy until you get hard again. I'm going to take a little nap while you do that. Wake me when you're ready to go again and we'll fuck some more."

As she dozed off immediately laying against me, I reflected that this could be quite a learning experience for me. I had very little experience in pussy eating, and my screwing experience was limited to getting on and humping as hard as I could, hoping to come. Perhaps this older, experienced and horny woman could show me a thing or two that I could benefit from. I'd only fucked twice in one night once so far, so that sounded good, too. At the least, it sounded like I would get a blow job out of it.

After my period of reflection, I reached for a boob that was near me and started playing with it and the nipple. That was fun, so I moved her gently off me and put her on her back, spreading her legs as she breathed heavily, deeply asleep with her head lolling off to one side. I reached for her pussy and explored it a bit, spreading the labia and looking at how things were arranged down there. Very interesting. It was like having a warm cadaver to experiment with.

As I did so, this was so kinky and erotic that my young cock started to wake up. I fingered her pussy for a bit as I explored, and then played with the boobs. I fantasized about slipping my cock into her mouth while she slept. Probably a bad idea.

My young cock was now fully erect. I gently nudged Lou as my cock bobbed. She wasn't waking up. Hmm. We were going to fuck again, so why not get started? Since I was about half drunk still, this made sense. I got between her legs and spread them enough, then pushed my cock into her sleeping pussy. I hoped she would not wake up mad or screaming. Maybe this was a bad idea. However, it felt damned good, so I started fucking a sleeping woman for the first time in my sex career.

After a minute of stroking, I started playing with her boobs while calling her name. After a bit, she started to rouse from the drunken nap and looked up at me with some confusion.

"What the ... Oh, hello. What's going on? Are you fucking me already? I guess you started without me. Mmm. That's a nice way to wake up. Or did I pass out while you were doing it?"

"No. I'm waking you up after your nap."

She reached up and started caressing my chest while yawning.

"How long was I out?'

"Oh, 15 minutes or so. I hope you don't mind that I started."

She nodded, taking stock of what was happening.

"No, that's okay. Wow! Your dick is as hard as a rock. It feels great! I'm glad you started. I was gonna have you eat my pussy first, but this is pretty okay for now."

I kept up a nice, slow pace.

"Glad you like it. I was afraid I was doing something wrong by starting while you were sleeping."

She laughed.

"I don't mind, but you might be careful of that in the future. Some women might consider it rape."

She saw my shocked face.

"It's okay! I invited you to do it, I was just expecting to be awake. Enough of that. Lift my legs up, to get in deeper. I like it deep, not everyone will."

"How's that?"

She closed her eyes.

"Real nice, sugar. Keep that up for a while. Does it feel good to you?"

"Oh, yeah!"

"Do you have a rubber?"

"Ah, no."

She nodded.

"Okay, just don't come in me until we are all done. I want some pussy eatin' later. You ever ate pussy?"

"Well, yeah. A couple of times."

She laughed sleepily.

"Don't you worry. Louise will show you what to do. You ever had a blow job?"

"Yes, Ma'am."

She laughed again and stroked my arms and chest as I pumped her.

"Call me Louise or Lou. Did those girls that blew you let you come in their mouth?"

This was a strange and intimate line of questions.

"No, they didn't."

"But you wanted to, right?"

"Yes, I did, very much so."

She laughed again and caressed my ass.

"I tell you what. You eat my pussy and make me come, then I'll let you come in my mouth. How's that?"

That sounded utterly fantastic! I tried to sound nonchalant.

"Yeah, that would be great."

"Okay, we'll do that. For right now, give me a nice, long fuck."

I fucked Lou smoothly and slowly for a good long while enjoying it immensely. This was probably the longest fuck yet for me. She seemed to like it, which was important to me. I was hoping I could make her come. I had gotten some good noises out of some of my young sex partners, I was just not sure an orgasm had taken place.

After several pleasant minutes, she opened her eyes, then reached up and put her hands together behind my neck and arched her back, stretching while I fucked her. It felt awesome.

"Mmm. That's nice, sugar. I almost fell asleep again, it felt so good. Now lift my legs up higher and you can start going faster and harder. Are you feeling like you want to come yet?"

I increased the rate and intensity a little and lifted her legs up. She helped by pulling her knees to her chest, which changed the way things felt.

"I wasn't feeling like I wanted to come yet, until you did that. That feels pretty good!"

She chuckled deep in her throat and moved her hands to my ass.

"I'm glad, honey. Let's see, no rubber, right?"

"Right."

"Okay, we have to find a place for you to come besides in my pussy. How about on my tits?"

"Wow! That sounds cool."

"Yeah, what you'll do is pull out, straddle my chest and put your cock between my tits, then I'll push them together around it, while you fuck my boobs. It's called a titty fuck. You ever done that?"

"No, I haven't even heard of that! It sounds very cool."

She laughed.

"I just felt your cock get even harder when I told you about it! Let me know when you are ready to come, and we'll do it. For now, this is feeling good to me. Go harder and faster!"

I ramped up the action and was feeling pretty good. Lou was enjoying it too, being very vocal and still drunk.

"Oh, yeah! That's it, stud! Give it to me harder! Faster! Harder! Yeah! Yeah!"

After a minute of that encouragement, I was reaching the boiling point. Lou felt it, too.

"Pull out and get between my titties! Now!"

I pulled my slimy cock out and laid it between her big boobs. Lou pushed them together, surrounding my dick. I started humping the titties, and it felt great. After about 30 seconds, I came, shooting rivulets of cum on her boobs and the base of her neck. She opened her mouth and caught a stray shot of semen on her lips, laughing delightedly.

I was panting with effort.

"That was so cool!"

She was still laughing.

"I'm glad I could show that to you! You'll never forget that!"

We both calmed down, and I went to get another warm, wet washcloth without being asked. We mopped up more cum and I wiped her down with a towel.

She looked at me expectantly.

"Okay, stud! Now let's get ready for some pussy eating."

I was still breathing hard.

"Don't we need a break?"

She laughed.

"Hell, no! We're gonna fuck all night! C'mon to the bathroom. You're gonna wash my pussy."

My ears perked up.

"Oh, really?"

"Yeah, I ain't had a shower since morning, so you're gonna give it a wash to get it all spiffed up before you start licking it. It'll be great, you'll love it!"

We went to the bathroom and prepared another wet washcloth with some soap. Lou stood next to the bathtub and put one foot up on the bathtub rim, effectively spreading her crotch open. I took the cloth and started gently washing her pussy and caressing her boobs and nipples with my other hand as she moaned with pleasure.

"Yeah! See? This is fun!"

I got the pussy nice and clean, then she turned around with her ass to me and looked over her shoulder at me, grinning drunkenly.

"Wash my butt crack, too! You never know what we might be doing."

"Gladly!"

I gave the butt crack a nice wash and patted Lou on the ass when I was done. She turned to me and took ahold of my cock.

"See? It's waking up already. You young studs can get it up in a hurry!"

I held her close and played with her boobs and ran a hand down to her pussy, which was nice and wet by now. Lou groaned with pleasure.

"Okay, stud. Now we are going to start the pussy licking. I'll tell you what to do."

She led me by the hand to the bed and flopped down on her back, spreading her legs.

"All right! Lay here next to me, I'm going to have you finger me to get started."

I lay next to her, and she took my hand and put it on her pussy.

"Now spread the lips with your first and third fingers. Good. Now use the big middle finger to do the tickling. Run it up here to the clit. The real name is clitoris, but we call it the clit. That's real sensitive and makes me real horny, so rub it gently. Yeah, that's it. Oooh! Good! Okay, you'll come back to that. Now stick that finger in, easy. This is not a pretend dick, it needs to rub on the upper side, Up on top, slide it back and forth rubbing the top of the inside, sort of towards my pubic hair. Yeah, ooohh! That's a good spot! Rub that lightly, then go back to the clit."

I did as requested, and Lou squirmed and squealed in delight.

"Good! You catch on quick! Now do that for a minute or two, then we'll replace the finger with your tongue."

After a time, I moved my face to her pussy and reveled in the smell of raw cunt. The aroma was intoxicating, and right there I decided that I wanted to do that to every woman I had sex with from then on. I moved my tongue to where my finger had been, and after licking the clit hesitantly pushed my tongue into the vaginal vault, trying to get where my finger had caused her pleasure. It must have been close enough, as Lou was going nuts.

"Oh, shit! Mmmm! Oh, YEAH! YEAH! OHHHH! AAHHH! OH, BABY! OH! AHHHH!"

After a couple of minutes of that intense action, Lou let out a howl of pleasure, the first time I had heard a woman have a loud, vocal orgasm. It was an experience I'll never forget.

After she calmed down, she found my cock and started stroking it.

"Oh yeah, stud! You made me come! That was great! Now, get on me and fuck me hard with this stiff cock! My pussy is tingling!"

I got on her and pushed right in. The hot, wet pussy felt fantastic. I started out slow, but she indicated this was not the time for that pace.

"Come on, sugar! Hard and fast! My pussy is tingling! I want your hard cock! Lift my legs up!"

I lifted her legs, and remembering something from a previous girlfriend, put her ankles on my shoulders and leaned forward, lifting her ass off the sheets, pounding away at her unprotected pussy. She screamed in pleasure as the erotic sound of flesh slapping as I rammed her pussy filled the room.

"OH! YEAH! OH, FUCK! GIVE IT TO ME, STUD! OOOHHH! YEAHHH!"

She clutched at my ass, pulling me deeper. After a couple of minutes of hard fucking, another howl escaped her mouth.

"AAAAHHHHH!!! Oh, YEAH!"

Her second orgasm shook the rafters, and I hoped any of my colleagues that were in adjoining rooms could hear us going at it.

She collapsed back into the bed, and I lowered her legs and caressed her boobs as she gasped for breath.

"OH! Man, that was good. Oh, sugar, you have what it takes. Mmm, mmm. Yes!"

I kept stroking her gently. Her eyes widened as she realized my stiff cock was still deep in her.

"Did you come?"

I shook my head no.

She grinned and sat up.

"Let me sit on the edge of the bed, sugar. You've earned a blow job all the way! Stand in front of me and bring me that hard cock!"

Lou took me in the mouth and commenced a wonderful blow job, bobbing up and own, rolling her tongue around my shaft and glans, cupping my balls with a free hand. It wasn't long before I felt the pressure rise.

"I'm gonna cum, Lou!"

Her eyes looked up into mine as she ramped up the suck job, and within seconds, I came in a woman's mouth for the first time in my life. Her eyes were locked onto mine as she slurped every drop of semen from my dick and swallowed it.

I almost passed out from the sensation, and I felt my knees wobble. I pulled out of her mouth, turned and sat down heavily on the bed beside her. I put my arm around her as she rested her head on my shoulder.

"Wow, Louise. Thanks!"

She grinned as she rubbed my bare thigh.

"No, thank you! That was a great orgasm you gave me. Twice! I loved it! You've got a gift. We'll have to do this again next week."

I smiled as I looked at her.

"I'm sorry, Lou. I'm only down here for a few more days."

She looked into my eyes.

"Then I'm glad we have tonight."

I was glad, too.

Lou went to the bathroom and came out, standing before me, stretching like a cat. Then she reached for my head and pulled it to her boobs, moving them up and down with my face in the middle. Pulling back, she grinned.

"Did you like that?"

"Yes! That was very cool. I'm experiencing all kinds of new things tonight."

I reached for her boobs and gave them a gentle squeeze, then leaned in and kissed the nipples several times. She liked that.

"Oh, yeah. That's nice. Let's try some more things you probably haven't done. Has a woman screwed you with her on top?"

I nodded.

"Once. It was fun."

"Did she get off while doing that?"

"I think so. She was pretty quiet."

Lou nodded wisely.

"Most women can get off riding you on top. It pushes against the clit, and your dick goes in real deep. How about on top facing away from you?"

"Nope. I didn't even think that was a position."

She laughed and sat on my lap, on her knees straddling me. Reaching down, she started stroking my cock.

"Yeah, on top facing you is the cowgirl, like a girl riding a horse. Facing away on top is reverse cowgirl. Get it?"

"Yep. Sounds interesting."

"It's fun. You can reach around and play with my clit while I'm riding you. How about doggie style?"

"Nope, heard of it but haven't done it."

"Oh, sugar. That will likely be your favorite."

She stroked my cock a moment more in silence, then gave it a squeeze. It must have been suitably hard. I was amazed it had regenerated in only a few minutes.

"Wow! You're hard again. Let's get back to it. I got some stuff for you to try."

Lou had me get on my back, and swung aboard, straddling my hips and easing my hard cock into as she sat down on it with a moan of pleasure. Once down all the way, she gave a wiggle that felt fantastic.

"Ah, I like it when I first get all the way down on your cock. Yeah!"

She rocked her hips back and forth, grinding her pussy into me.

"Push up into me!"

I did and was rewarded with a loud moan as she closed her eyes. She moved her hips forward and back, while bracing herself against my shoulders as I humped up into her. It felt natural to play with her boobs since they were swaying in front of my face, so I caressed them and kissed the nipples.

After a few minutes of activity, she was getting wound up.

"AAHH! Yeah! OH, YEAH! MMM! COME ON! OH, YEAH!"

I kept up my thrusting into her and saw a look of concentration on her face. I was playing with her boobs and kissing the nipples when she had a request.

"Bite my nipples, stud! Bite 'em!"

Well, that was new for me, so I gently nibbled the cute little nipples, which were standing straight out.

"Harder! Bite them harder!"

I bit down some more, which was what she needed.

"OOOHH! FUCK! OH! OH, GODDAMN! OH! OH! AAHHH!"

She sat straight up and put her hands behind her own head, tilting her head back as her hips gyrated on my cock, then let out a loud howl of delight.

After a minute, she regained her composure.

"Oh yeah! That was nice! Okay, I'm gonna climb off and show you the reverse cowgirl. You doing okay? Need to come yet?"

"I'm good for a while!"

She climbed off and got back on my dick facing away from me. This was my first experience with fucking from behind, and I liked it a lot.

Lou started rocking her hips back and forth, and I pushed up into her without being told.

"Reach around and play with my clit!"

I found that I could reach her pussy, and it was fun to play with her clit while I fucked her.

"This is fun, Lou!"

"Yeah, but most women won't come like this. Better with the regular cowgirl."

She rode me for a while, bending way over and bracing herself on my ankles. I had to admit, it was cool.

"Okay, I'll climb off and get on my hands and knees. Get behind me and slip it in."

She turned around and went to her elbows and knees, facing away from me with her ass in the air. I moved in behind and put my stiff meat near where I thought it went. She guided it into the labia, and I pushed in. It felt great.

"Oh, Lou. That's nice."

"Put your legs outside of mine, that will keep me from sliding around."

I did as instructed, it was a lot better.

"This feels great, Lou!"

"Good, sugar. Do it slow for a bit, then crank it up. You're gonna love it."

I admired her ass and back for a while as I fucked her slowly, holding her by the waist. Then I cranked it up and enjoyed watching her ass jiggle and her boobs sway as I pounded into her.

"Yeah! This is fucking fantastic!"

"Do it hard for a minute, then I'm gonna move you so you can come."

"Okay. Where am I going?"

She turned her head around and grinned at me.

"Get the lotion. You're gonna come in my ass!"

"What! I've never done that!"

She laughed.

"I like it, and I'm showing you new stuff, so I figured what the hell. I'm still a little drunk, so it's a good time to fuck me in the ass! Get the lotion and lube up my asshole by putting lotion on your finger and pushing it into my asshole. Then lube up your dick."

I did as instructed, my cock getting as excited as I was. The feel of my finger in her ass was fantastic.

"Okay, ease it up to the hole and push in real easy. You'll feel it stretch real slow, then you'll go right in. Then it's like doggie style, except it hurts so good!"

I pushed the head of my dick into her puckered asshole, and as she said, I could feel the anal sphincter yield and then I was in. I started an easy fucking as she groaned and moaned. My first anal sex episode was amazing.

"Oh, wow Lou! It's so tight and sexy!"

She liked it, too.

"Oh, damn! That feels so good! Do it harder!"

I ramped it up and was getting close to coming.

"Ahh! I'm gonna come!"

"Yeah, sugar! Fill my ass with your cum! Yeah!"

With that encouragement, I shot a load into her ass and groaned mightily.

"Damn, Lou! That was fucking great!"

She laughed.

"I like it, but a lot of women won't. Leave your dick in for a minute, it's cool to feel it shrink."

I did and stroked her ass as she waited patiently. Then I pulled out easy and heard a plop as my dick came out. A dribble of cum ran out of her ass. It was quite the sight.

"Get me a tissue, sugar. I don't want to drip on the way to the bathroom."

"You got it."

She went and cleaned up the mess. I went in and thoroughly washed my cock. I looked in the mirror and shook my head. I was getting the full treatment and was loving it. Back in bed, she was ready to sleep.

"Lou, I have to get up early ..."

"It'll be fine, honey. I want to spend the night here if it's okay."

"Well ... sure. Why not? It's really late and we are still a little drunk."

She smiled at me and held out her arms.

We turned out the light and went to sleep.

When my alarm went off at 6:00 am, she looked me straight in the eye and reached for my cock, stroking it until it got hard, which did not take long. I caressed her boobs while she was stroking me. Then she rolled on her back and pulled me to her. Without a word, I entered her while we were looking into each other's eyes and fucked her slowly for several minutes, then we began to get hot at the same time.

I quickened my pace as she lifted her knees while stroking my hair and ass. I ramped up the intensity and after several wonderful minutes we both climaxed at the same time as we again looked into each other's eyes, with her back arched and pussy spasming as she shuddered from the force of the orgasm, this one quiet as her mouth was wide open in a silent scream. I groaned heavily and shot a load of cum into her pussy for the first time.

We lay together, breathing hard. She caressed my back and legs as I kissed her boobs, and finally, her mouth. After a passionate kiss, we smiled at each other, and she silently got out of bed.

Lou wiped herself off, dressed quickly and left the room without looking at me. I could hear the Cadillac starting and I pulled the curtain aside and watched it pull away.

I entered the shower and turned the water on hot, standing there under the stinging spray, recuperating. Thinking about the events of the night and morning, I vowed never to forget her.

I never have. Here's to you, Louise, wherever you may be, taking young men to new heights of sexual experience.

Jackie

For this encounter, I was in Canon City, Colorado in February. At 24 years old, I was on my way from one Air Force duty assignment in California to my next in Indiana, and I had to stop in Canon City to take care of something. I was staying at a Holiday Inn, which usually was an okay chain. Leaving town tomorrow, I was going to work my way over to I-25 and then south and then east to visit a friend in Enid, Oklahoma before heading to Indiana.

At about 1800 (6 pm for you civilians) as I came back into the hotel from my obligation ready for a drink, the friendly desk clerk reminded me that it was ladies' night in the hotel bar.

"It's pretty popular. There will be lots of young women there."

I nodded gratefully. It had been a while since I had relieved my biological urges. I had been wrapped up with a technical school and had concentrated on doing well at the school instead of getting laid. It had paid off; I was a distinguished graduate of the school. Also recently divorced, I was a bit lonesome for some female companionship. Maybe one of the locals would give it up for a one-night stand with a stranger passing through. Like me.

"Thanks, I'll check it out."

I already had eaten, so I changed into a nice shirt and slacks and watched TV until the event started. Entering the bar, it was indeed crowded with locals. I got a drink at the bar and started shooting the breeze with the guy on the bar stool next to me.

After trading conversation about the weather and the town, he indicated that the local chicks were hard to break away from their friends. All they wanted was to have guys buy them drinks and dance with them. I surveyed the scene and agreed. There wasn't a whole lot of hooking up happening. Oh, well. I might as well give it a try.

I danced with a few different ladies and then ended up focusing on a chubby one who seemed interested in me. Dressed casually, she was about my age and had shoulder-length brown and blonde hair, which we used to call dirty blonde. As we danced the first time, her hips pushed against me, perhaps innocently. The next time we danced, she did it again, twice. The third time she pushed against me once, and I sprung a boner. Rubbing against it on purpose later, she smiled. She was a prick teaser. I repeated the dance thing a few more times and sat with her and her friends for a while, chatting them up.

My friend at the bar was right. I couldn't break one of these chicks free with a chisel. Rather than waste money pouring drinks into them, I leaned over to my chubby friend and whispered in her ear that if she was lonely at the end of the evening, she could look me up in room 409. I stood, said goodnight to all, waved at my acquaintance at the bar, and headed for my room.

Back in my room, I stripped down to a tee shirt and shorts, then watched a cop show on TV, then the 11 o'clock news to see what the weather would be like for my drive the next day. Fully informed, I then turned out my light. It had been a nonproductive evening.

Not 10 minutes later, I heard a rapping at my door. Curious, I got up and looked through the peephole and saw the chubby chick I had danced with.

I opened the door. Jackie was smiling shyly.

"Can I come in?"

I shrugged.

"Sure."

She came in and we sat together on the end of the bed. I looked at her, waiting for some kind of sign. She gave me one.

"I thought we could go to breakfast."

"There's nothing better than going to breakfast after a night of drinking. Why did you come by to pick me up?"

She looked at me shyly.

"Well, I thought you were nice and wanted to go with you."

I had to laugh.

"I bought you some drinks and danced with you, did you think I would buy your breakfast, too?"

She nodded and smiled.

"Something like that. I hope so."

I decided to be bold.

"I'd be glad to do that, but I'm going to have something in return."

She looked me in the eye.

"And what would that be?"

It was my turn to grin.

"After you teased me by pushing your hips into me and rubbing against my boner, I think you know what I want."

Reaching for her hand, I put it on my cock outside my shorts. She smiled and nodded.

"I thought that was it. Fair enough, I was teasing you. I guess that backfired on me."

She gave my limp cock a squeeze, making up her mind.

"Okay. You want it before we go to breakfast, I guess?"

I was surprised. Really? Was it going to be that easy to get laid?

"Yep, that's what I want."

She nodded again and stood up and started quickly taking her clothes off. Within a minute, she had taken off her shoes, removed her pants and underwear, then sat back on the end of the bed and reached for my shorts and my cock.

"I suppose you want me to blow you to get you hard."

"That would be nice."

"Okay. Stand up in front of me."

I did. She slid my shorts down, took hold of my exposed dick, and without preamble, started an excellent blow job. I was impressed. How did this small-town chick learn her way around a cock?

Within a few minutes, my dick was standing at attention. She must have felt it was hard enough, as she pulled back and lay back on her elbows with her legs spread, hanging off the edge of the bed, and looked me in the eye.

I was looking at a half-naked woman who was ready to fuck me within five minutes of entering my room. Why can't it always be this simple? I leaned over to my suitcase, fished out a condom, and put it on while she watched. When I was ready, I stood at the end of the bed between her spread legs. She was at the perfect fucking height.

With a smile, she bent down and took my condom-coated cock into her mouth to give it some lubrication. Then she pulled the head of my cock to the entrance of her vagina. I reached down and put a finger in her pussy to see if things were ready. It was not sopping wet, but slippery enough that additional lubrication was not needed. I added another finger and smeared pussy juice on the labia and the end of my condom. I put the head of my meat missile up against the lips, and using my hand, rubbed it up and down to spread the wetness around. With the saliva and pussy juice, the condom was good to go.

I pushed into her vagina and was pleased with the feeling. It was just a little snug, nice and warm, and had sufficient lubrication. Nice pussy. Jackie closed her eyes and sighed, giving a slight moan as my cock hit bottom. As I wiggled my hips and arranged myself between her chubby thighs, I admired her pubic hair and pussy. I felt lucky to be there. My goal of getting some pussy on this overnight stop was being fulfilled, and it felt good.

I started stroking into Jackie slowly while holding onto her thick waist, noticing that she was still clothed from the waist up. She had only shed enough clothing to facilitate the quick fuck. She must really want to go to breakfast. Maybe she was hungry.

"You feel nice, Jackie."

She lay there motionless, holding my hips as I pumped my stiff cock into her. She was looking up at me now, watching my face without expression as I fucked her. Her pussy felt good, even if she wasn't moving. It was better than jacking off. I realized that this was the first pussy my cock had been in besides my young wife, well make that ex-wife now. Anyway, it had been two years since I had been in another woman. I told Jackie that, and she gave me a small smile as I pumped her.

I decided I wanted to see her boobs. Reaching around her back, I managed to unhook her bra and lifted the sweater.

"I want to see your titties."

She smiled and lifted the shirt and bra higher to free the boobs, and they bobbed into view. I placed a hand on each tit and gave them a gentle squeeze. The big girl boobs were soft and warm, with pert pink nipples that I tweaked.

After a minute, she chuckled and commented.

"You must be a boob man. After you played with them, your dick got even harder!"

I grinned.

"I do like boobs."

She smiled and squeezed my ass cheeks as I continued to fuck her, while still looking me in the eyes.

After a few pleasant minutes of fucking, my biological back pressure built up, and I picked up the pace to a faster pumping rhythm. Her big girl boobs jiggled enticingly as I plowed her hard. With my balls feeling that ejaculation was inevitable, I fucked her harder and faster until I shot several long spurts of cum into the condom.

"Mmm. Thanks, Jackie. That was nice," I moaned.

She smiled again, and as I pulled out of her and stood up, she got up and went to the bathroom. I heard the sound of running water, and presently she came out with her sweater and bra in place and donned the rest of her clothes.

"Well, now I suppose we can go to breakfast after you get dressed."

I smiled. She had a one-track mind. Fuck the stranger, get rewarded with food.

"Yes, I suppose so. Let me get rid of this used condom. Want to go to the IHOP next door?"

"That would be great."

After we were both dressed, we walked to the IHOP. It was freezing cold, and the wind made it feel colder. After placing our order and sipping coffee, we started to compare notes.

She asked, "What was your name again?"

I smiled. She had fucked me and didn't even know my name. This was developing into a perfect one-night stand.

"Dirk."

"I'm Jackie. Tell me about yourself, Dirk."

"I'm from California. I'm in the Air Force and am on my way to Indiana for my next assignment."

She nodded.

"Are you married? Any kids?"

"I just got out of a marriage; I don't think I'll be doing that again. No kids. How about you?"

"I'm divorced. One small kid. I don't think I am ready for anything long-term right now. I work at Walmart, stocking shelves until something better comes along. I was born here and went to school here, but I kind of want to get away."

I looked around. We had taken a booth well away from any of the other customers.

"Well, you must have learned something from that marriage. You give a great blow job."

She blushed.

"Thanks. I don't mind doing it for men I like, so I must like you."

"I'm flattered. After breakfast, I'd like you to suck my dick again."

"Aww, Dirk. I thought we were just going to have a quickie and go to breakfast."

I laughed.

"I'm ready for more. Screwing you felt pretty good to me. How about it?"

She nodded and blushed again.

"I suppose so. I didn't get a lot out of that quickie. Not your fault, I wanted to get going. I don't mind telling you that I like your body, you are so slim and fit. It's a nice change from the local fat dudes that want to fuck me. I'd like to do it again with you, nice and slow. We can go to my place and take our time after we eat, and maybe I'll give you some more head."

We finished breakfast, which was my treat of course. She needed a ride to her small studio apartment that looked like it used to be a seedy motel. Upon entering, I noticed it was a mess. She took off her coat and turned to me, putting her arms around me. She wanted to kiss, I wanted to fuck. I compromised by kissing for a while as my hands roamed her body.

After kissing for a couple of minutes, she was ready to move to the next step. We undressed and climbed into her bed. She caressed my chest and arms, while I played with her big boobs and ran my hands over her chubby body. I admired the soft mounds as I caressed them and kissed the nipples. She moaned softly and spread her legs for me to play with her.

I put my hand on her pussy and then played with her clit. She moaned and exclaimed.

"Oh, that feels good."

I smiled.

"Haven't you had anyone play with your clit before?"

She squirmed.

"Not much, usually the man just sticks his finger in me, then the dick, then humps real fast until they come."

I laughed.

"Your clit needs attention, and then you need to be fingered correctly and then fucked lovingly."

She smiled at me while stroking my hair.

"I'd like that. I've never really had an orgasm before, so I'd like to try."

I was surprised.

"Never had an orgasm?"

She shook her head as her eyes closed while my finger gently circled her clit.

"Well, I've felt really good several times, but never had something like I read about in the magazines. What you are doing feels real good right now."

I felt that it was time to be bold again. What the hell, this was a one-night deal. Might as well go for broke.

"I'll make you a deal. If I can get you to have an orgasm, I get to come in your mouth, and you have to swallow my cum."

Her eyes flew open, and she looked at me, shocked.

"Wow! That's pretty out there! I've had guys come in my mouth, I didn't especially like it, let alone swallow. Damn! You California guys are pretty demanding."

I gave her clit a nice tickle. She moaned and made up her mind.

"Okay! Deal! But I have to agree that I had a real orgasm, not just feeling good."

"That sounds reasonable."

She put her arms around my neck, and her hips squirmed a little as she smiled at me.

"But no matter what, you're gonna fuck me again, right?"

I smiled at her.

"That's the plan."

She closed her eyes again.

"Good. I like the sound of that. Work your magic."

With the negotiation behind us, I ran my finger into her vaginal vault and rubbed the upper portion of the tunnel of love. Louise had shown me that, and although I did not at the time understand where the G spot was, I knew that it usually got a positive reaction. Jackie moaned again.

With my free hand, I squeezed and caressed her boobs, playing with the erect nipples and then kissed and licked them. She liked that but liked the vaginal attention better.

I pulled my wet finger out and used it to circle her clit and gently tickle it. Jackie moaned and her hips moved. For several minutes, I went back and forth between her clit and pussy, as I gave her big boobs lots of attention. The sounds she made indicated to me that she was close. I decided to see what my tongue could do. If I could get her wound up, when I gave her the dick she would probably orgasm.

Moving my head down to her meaty pussy lips, I ran my tongue up and down them for a minute, then used the end of my tongue to stimulate her clit, drawing circles around it. Then I stuck my tongue in the vaginal vault where my finger had been and got a great reaction.

"Oh! Nobody's ever done that to me! Ah! It feels so good!"

The tongue action was sending her over the top. She was moaning and groaning nonstop now and getting vocal.

"Oh! Wow! That feels good! Oh! Yeah! Mmm. Oh, yeah!"

She was really close. I used my spare hand and gave one of the nipples a hard pinch. Then I took that hand and reached for her butt crack and circled her anus with my fingertip. That put her over the edge.

"OH! OH! AAHHHHH!! OH, THAT'S AMAZING! OH! OH! OH!"

Her back arched, and she grabbed my head with both hands and pulled my face into her pussy.

"AAAHHH!!!"

She let out a low howl of ecstasy, and I wondered what the neighbors thought. Hopefully, their TVs were on an action show. After the orgasm went through her, she collapsed back on the bed, panting. I looked at her and smiled. I was going to come in her mouth. But first, some fucking.

I rolled over and got between her legs as she stared up at me with her mouth open and her eyes unfocused. She was still dazed from the orgasm. I moved my erect cock to her glistening labia and split the lips with the head of my cock and pushed all the way into her. I paused and reached down to put some pressure on her clit.

Jackie regained her senses, opened her eyes, and started babbling as I fucked her slowly. She put one hand behind my head with the other on my ass.

"Oh, wow! That was incredible! That's the best feeling ever! Man, how do you do that?"

I smiled at her.

"Just practice, I guess. How are you feeling now?"

She grinned at me.

"I'm feeling like I am ready to suck you off! You deserve it! But my pussy is still tingling. Is that normal?"

"Yeah, that's good news. Lift your knees up and let me get deeper and see if that still feels good."

"Okay!" She lifted her chubby thighs up and held her knees to her chest. I drilled her deep, and she reacted.

"Oh, shit! That is still feeling really good! Oh!"

I gave it to her harder. She immediately reacted.

"Wow! Your cock is so hard! Oh, man! Wow!"

I decided to go for broke. Lifting her ankles up even with my shoulders, I spread her legs as far as I could. I pounded her pussy hard and fast. After a couple of minutes, she came unglued.

"OH! OH! OH, SHIT! IT'S ALMOST THERE AGAIN!"

Encouraged, I pounded her as hard and fast as I could, pile-driving her exposed pussy. She was pulling on my ass with both hands.

"AH! AH! AH! OH, YEAH!"

I looked her in the eyes as her boobs jiggled from the pounding.

"Say my name when you come!"

"OH! YES! OH, DIRK! OH, DIRK! I'M COMING AGAIN, DIRK! AAAHHHH!!"

Jackie let out a scream of pleasure and her pussy spasmed around my rock hard cock. It was all I could do to keep from coming, but my dick had an appointment with her mouth. I pulled out and knelt in front of her.

"Suck my cock! Now!"

She sat up and while panting, got my dick in her mouth and started a rapid blow job just in time. I put a hand behind her head and pulled her to me to keep her from escaping and pushed my cock deep into her throat. My head went back, my eyes closed, and I felt hot lava rising from my balls. With a powerful spasm, I groaned loudly as I shot load after load of sticky cum into her mouth and throat.

Opening my eyes, I looked down at her as her eyes went up to mine. She was waiting.

"Swallow! Swallow my cum!"

With her eyes on mine, I could see her throat work as she swallowed, and I felt her throat contract around my cock. She had swallowed my load of cum. Then her tongue circled my shaft and glans as she licked it clean.

After a bit, she pulled back and wiped a trace of semen off her mouth with the back of her hand. She grinned, still breathing hard.

"That wasn't so bad! After two orgasms, I hardly noticed it."

I held her head gently and stroked her hair. After a bit, I lay next to her. She got up and went into her tiny bathroom. I heard the water running and the sound of her spitting. Coming back to bed, she covered us up with the sheet and blanket, and snuggled next to me, tucking her face into my neck as she sighed with pleasure.

"Well, now I know what an orgasm is, thanks to you."

I caressed her plump ass and the back of her legs.

"I'm glad I could help."

After a minute, she had a question.

"Why did you want me to say your name when I came?"

I laughed.

"Up in my room, you didn't even know my name when I fucked you the first time. I wanted you to remember who made you come."

She laughed into my neck.

"I'm not going to forget that! Or you! My first orgasm and I've never been fucked so hard in my life. It was fantastic!"

After a few minutes, I started feeling sleepy.

"Well, Jackie, I'd better go."

She raised her head and nodded, fighting off a yawn, then pulled me close.

"Stay the night, Dirk. Please? I want some more screwing and pussy licking later, but I'm sleepy now."

This was pretty comfortable. And the prospect of more nooky? Hmm. Time to be bold again.

"Well, I'll do that for you on a condition."

She rose up with a smile and looked at me.

"Conditions, again! Really? What is it this time?"

"I'll eat you out again if you blow me and then let me fuck you in your ass and cum in your butt."

She shook her head as she grinned.

"Dirk, my friend, you are one kinky dude. I agree."

I had to laugh.

"That was too easy. Let me guess, you like it in the ass, right?"

She nodded and laughed.

"You guessed right, but you already agreed, so no changing your mind."

"That's fine. It'll be fun. Nap time for now?"

"Yeah, let's get a good nap and then have some more fun."

We slept for a couple of hours. It was about 0430 (4:30 am for you civilians) when I awoke and had to hit the head, and when I climbed back in the bed she roused.

Jackie stretched and yawned.
"Is it time for early morning sex yet?"
I smiled and played with her boobs.
"I could be talked into that."
She rolled into me and hugged me tightly.

"Dirk, I want some oral sex, but don't feel real fresh down there. Let me take a shower before we do it, okay? I'd be embarrassed otherwise."
"I'm real handy in the shower, I'll join you."

She perked up.

"That sounds like fun!"

"I have to warn you, I'm prone to shower boners when bathing with women."

She grinned.

"That sounds like even more fun! Let's go!"

We enjoyed a nice soapy shower, washing each other's private parts. Sure enough, my cock sprung to attention, and she soaped it slowly and lovingly.

"Wow! You weren't kidding! You are ready to rock!"

"As advertised. Have you ever had shower sex?"

She laughed.

"Why no, Mister Dirk. I have not. What all is involved in that?"

"It's easy. Face away from me and bend at the waist. I recommend you brace yourself by placing your hands on your knees."

She turned away and bent over as instructed.

"Okay, try and keep my hair dry. What's next?"

"Now I slip my salami into your wet pussy."

She laughed again. I slipped my meat into her and gave her several good strokes, which caused her to yelp and giggle.

"Oh, my! That is fun!"

After a minute of that, I pulled out.

"Now turn around and put my dick between your nice big wet and soapy boobs, squeeze them together, and rub it."

She did so and looked up at me.

"You have the best ideas!"

After a minute, I called a halt.

"We'd better dry off and get back in bed before I come on your boobs."

She looked at me with a sly grin.

"If I let you come on my boobs, would you be able to finish what we planned on earlier?"

That was a great question. My dick was really happy where it was.

"Umm. Yes. I will rest up while eating your pussy, and then be able to take care of your ass after a while."

Without a word, she increased the rate of boob rubbing, and in a minute, I announced imminent ejaculation.

"Ahhh! I'm about to cum, Jackie!"

My cock erupted onto her big boobs and the base of her neck as she used her hand to guide the discharge. I felt my knees get weak as spasms of cum dribbled out after the main event.

"That was nice! Thanks!"

She laughed and stood up.

"At least we're in the right place to clean me up! Help me wash your cum off my boobs!"

"Yes, Ma'am!"

A short time later, she was once again semen free and we toweled off and went back to bed. Snuggling, we chatted a bit, and then she grew impatient.

"When are you going to get on with the oral sex?"

I tried to look surprised.

"Oh, did you want to try and come again?"

She scowled fiercely and punched my shoulder.

"Yes! Quit stalling!"

"Ow! Well, if you're going to start playing rough ..."

I roughly pulled Jackie over on top of me as she squealed and laughed. I sat her up and started pulling her to my head.

"Get up here and sit on my face and I'll give you what you want!"

She giggled as she squirmed forward, straddling my head with her big thighs, and soon I had a face full of pussy. She was sitting straight up, bracing herself on the headboard of the bed. I put my hands under her ass and did some fine tuning of her position and put my tongue to work.

My nose was near her clit, and I used my fingers to spread the hood of skin over the small protrusion and gave it an exploratory lick and a very tender nibble. This had the desired effect as Jackie moaned deeply and I heard a sharp intake of breath. I gave the clit some attention, and then worked my tongue down the labia, enjoying the aroma of freshly washed cunt.

Working my tongue into the vaginal vault, I sought the area where I would get the most reaction, on the roof of the vagina. This was a hit with Jackie, as she squirmed her hips into my face and groaned with pleasure. For several minutes I kept up the attention to the vagina, alternating with visits to the clit for variety. She was squirming and moaning constantly now, and to help things along I reached up to squeeze her nipples and fondle her boobs. She was on the verge of orgasm, her third. I needed to push her over the edge.

Reaching a hand to the pussy, I circled the clit with a finger as I licked it gently, then ran the finger near her sopping wet vagina to get it good and wet. I reached around her plump butt and found her anus and started circling it and penetrating it a little. That had the desired effect, and Jackie very loudly launched into an orgasm.

"OH! OH! OH! OH, DIRK! I'M COMING! OH, DIRK! OH! AAAHHHHH!!"

With a soft scream, she took hold of my head with her hands and pulled my face hard up into her wet pussy while grinding her hips into my face. For a moment there I couldn't breathe, but I knew she would let go of me in a minute. After a few moments, it was over, and she let go of my head and again braced herself on the headboard as she collapsed onto me.

Panting, she squirmed her body down me until she was lying on top of me with her face next to mine. I had a big erection going that I positioned between her meaty thighs at her crotch and gently stroked between them, which was kind of fun. She leaned up to kiss me, then backed off, laughing.

"Your face is a mess!"

Indeed, my face had a lot of her pussy juice and my saliva on it.

"It's worth it to make you feel good."

She climbed off me, went to the bathroom, came back with a damp cloth, and gently wiped my face. Noticing my boner, she stroked it gently and smiled.

"Ready for the next step?"

I nodded.

"Oh, yeah! I got pretty horny during all that. Do you have any Vaseline or lotion?"

I've never met a woman who did not have either product at the bedside. She reached to the nightstand and pulled out a bottle of lotion.

"Let's use this."

"Great. Now get on your hands and knees. I take it you've done this before?"

"Yeah, several times. Usually when I'm drunk. Since I'm almost sober now, this may be different."

She rolled over and assumed the position. I knelt behind her and started lubing up her asshole, outside and in. She gasped when my finger first went in.

I moved up and positioned my cock at her pussy and started entering her as she giggled.

"Wrong hole!"

I had heard that one before.

"First I want some of that sweet pussy, doggie style!"

"You say the nicest things. That feels good, just don't cum in there."

"Got it!"

I started a nice fast fuck, enjoying watching her ass jiggle as I plowed her. Her big boobs were swinging wildly, and I used one hand to corral one while I held her waist with the other. It felt nice, and we both enjoyed a few minutes of nice fucking.

I pulled out reluctantly.

"Let's get to the main event."

Taking more lotion and lubing up my cock, I moved the head of my dick to her wrinkled asshole and plugged the hole.

"Ready?"

She nodded, her hands clutching the sheet in anticipation of the feeling.

I pushed into the anal sphincter and felt it slowly yield and stretch as Jackie drew in a breath and tensed up. I patted her ass and waited a minute for her to relax, then pushed in past the sphincter and felt her breath normally.

"Oh, Dirk! Damn! That kind of hurts but I like it!"

I pushed in some more, and when I had most of my dick in her, started an easy pumping rhythm. She moaned and tossed her head as I fucked her but did not complain. I guess she did like it.

Soon, I felt my balls loading up and started going a little faster. She picked up on that right away.

Speaking with effort as I pumped her, she said, "You can go harder and faster to come if you want."

I ramped up the rate and depth as I admired the sight of my cock going in and out of her ass. I had her by the shoulders pulling her to me hard as the moment neared. All at once, my personal volcano erupted, and I shot a load of cum into her ass as I groaned loudly. I stopped the pumping motion and stayed in her as I felt my cock spasm as a few more spurts went into her. She wiggled her butt into me, which felt great.

Enjoying the moment as my dick started shrinking, I pulled back slowly and was gratified to see a big dribble of cum leaking from her ass.

"Whew! That was great, Jackie! Was that what you wanted?"

She laughed as she reached back to her leaking ass with the washcloth.

"Oh, yeah! That checked off one of my desires. It's different when you're sober. Not bad, just different."

Jackie held the cloth to her ass and waddled to the bathroom. When she came out, I went in and gave my cock a thorough wash and dry. Back in bed, she wanted to snuggle for a bit. It was the least I could do.

After a nice interval of snuggling, she rose up and looked at me.

"We should get up. I have to get ready for work soon. Sorry, but I don't have anything to give you for breakfast. I could make coffee if you want."

I looked at my watch, it was past 6am.

"I suppose I should go back to the hotel and check out, then get on the road if I'm going to make Oklahoma today."

I got dressed as she lay in bed and watched me.

"Dirk? Am I ever going to see you again?"

I looked at her and shook my head.

"Not likely, Jackie."

She smiled and hugged her knees to her chest, looking thoughtful.

After getting dressed, I went to the door. She came to me, still naked, and put her arms around me as she looked up into my face.

"It was nice meeting you, Dirk. Thanks for a great night."

I kissed her.

"It was my pleasure."

I squeezed her naked ass as she giggled.

"Mine too!"

I let her go and went out the door. I was two steps away when I heard my name being called. I turned around. She was peeking around the open door, smiling.

"I just wanted to say your name again."

I smiled back at her, then turned and walked out to my car. As I started the engine, I noticed a layer of light snow and frost on the windshield. I shivered in the cold light of dawn. Damn, it was cold in Colorado! My nuts ached from the multiple ejaculations, but I was ready to get back on the road and had enjoyed my night in Canon City. I would never come back.

Veronica

It was still early in my career, and I was in the active duty Air Force serving as an inflight refueling operator in the grade of Staff Sergeant, stationed at a base in Northern Indiana. At the moment, I was in a historic pub in England's village of Feltwell. More specifically, I was engaged in having sex with my navigator's British cousin, whom I had sitting on the sink with her skirt up and her stockings down behind a locked door in the lavatory (also called a loo) as I stood in front of her stroking my hard cock into her wet pussy as her father and cousin were drinking in the noisy bar. Veronica was trying to stifle sounds of pleasure to avoid discovery as I rammed into her while she clung to exposed pipes on the wall. I was nearing climax, and that built up load of cum had to go somewhere, anywhere but into her vagina.

I had come to be in this situation by a fortuitous turn of events. My aircrew scheduling office had offered up a short notice 30-day trip to England. This was a plum trip and would get me out of the steamy Indiana summer at the air base north of Indianapolis. Barbara, the lady I was seeing at the time, was not real pleased that I was leaving the country on such short notice. I'd have to deal with her when I got back. I would be filling in for another crew member that had become ill, so I went to meet his crew and became a part of their planning process. On a Monday evening, we took off directly for RAF Mildenhall, UK. During the flight, the navigator was telling me that he had family near our destination in England.

"Dirk, my uncle lives in Feltwell, about a 30 minute drive from Mildenhall. I'm planning on seeing him and my cousin soon after I get there. Why don't you come with me?"

I was curious, so as we roared over the dark Atlantic in the middle of the night, I asked some questions.

"How did your uncle end up living in England?"

Mike, the navigator, shook his head and laughed.

"He was in the Air Force stationed at RAF Lakenheath and met an English girl. They fell in love, got married, and when Fred's enlistment was up, he stayed there. He got a civil service job at the base and has assimilated into the community. They had a daughter, who's my cousin. I've only seen them a few times, but I wrote them about this trip and they responded, very excited to see me. I'll call them when we get there and arrange a visit. You should come and entertain my cousin while I catch up with Uncle Fred. I don't really have anything in common with her. Her name is Veronica, and she's about your age."

I was 24 years old at the time. The thought of meeting an English girl was interesting. I'd met a few English ladies, but they were the bar fly types at the base club and as such were not desirable.

"Okay, you're on. I'll go with you and meet the cousin."

We found England with no difficulty and after some in processing we flew a couple of local flights over Europe on Wednesday and Friday, and on Friday afternoon Mike and I headed to Feltwell on a bus, armed with a map and directions to walk to Fred's house when the bus dropped us off. We were off duty for the weekend, so this was a good time to meet Uncle Fred and Cousin Veronica.

Mike and I found the house with no issues, and we met Fred and his wife Maggie. They were charming and friendly, inviting us in for tea and scones as a snack waiting for Veronica to join us after she got off work. Soon Fred was plying us with whisky and started in on family stories about his brother and Mike when he was young. After a while, Veronica arrived.

She was, as the Brits say, a stunner. With dark red hair framing her oval face, and green eyes over great cheekbones with a spray of freckles and fashionable glasses, she was dressed stylishly in a long-sleeved sweater and mini skirt with dark stockings. Veronica (call me Roni) was of medium height and build, with shapely legs and the promise of a nice rack hidden by her sweater. She was British all the way, from her accent and speech to her mannerisms. I was entranced. She must have been also as she was staring at me with her eyes flashing while she smiled and blushed.

"Hello, Cousin Mike! It's lovely to see you!"

They embraced, then she turned to me.

"Who's your friend?"

Mike introduced us, and she smiled as she extended her hand. I swear there was a spark between us as we shook hands. She blushed again as her eyes sparkled with excitement.

"It's a pleasure to meet you, Dirk. I'm glad you came with my Cousin."

"I'm glad to meet you, Roni. I've been looking forward to this visit."

Roni smiled again and took a small whisky to sip on while Fred and Mike reminisced. Soon Maggie called us for supper, and Roni sat next to me at the small table. Her knee found itself against mine several times, as she smiled at me. I was beginning to think there might be a possibility of romance in the offing.

After dinner, Fred wanted to take us to his local pub for a drink and darts. Maggie abstained, so as we walked the three blocks to the 'local' Mike and Fred walked ahead as Roni and I walked together. Soon Roni slipped her hand into mine as she looked at me and smiled and blushed again. Letting the others get ahead, she spoke softly to me, so her Dad and Cousin could not hear.

"Dirk, I got the strangest feeling when I met you and touched your hand the first time."

I had an inkling of what was coming next.

"What's that, Roni?"

She smiled again.

"I had this sudden urge to have sex with you."

I smiled back at her as my loins stirred. Glancing up at Fred and Mike getting farther away from us, I replied.

"I felt it too, Roni. What shall we do about it?"

She laughed as she squeezed my hand and pressed close to me.

"I suppose we will be sneaking off to either my flat or your room on base. I almost can't wait!"

It was my turn to laugh.

"That's not a bad choice. Let's enjoy the pub and see where the night takes us."

She smiled again.

"Kiss me, Dirk."

I looked up at the men we were following.

"Right here?"

She stopped.

"Yes, quickly. I want to see what it's like."

I turned to her and in a second, we were kissing standing up on the street. Her tongue found its way into my mouth for a quick exploration, then we were back to walking, both flushed with sexual excitement.

She looked at me and shook her head.

"My God, I feel like I'm on fire. Let's make excuses and head to my flat!"

Part of me seconded that idea, but we were at the pub entrance, with Fred eyeing us.

"Now then, what have you two been up to?"

In my head I formed a thought. Well, Fred, your daughter and I can't wait to ditch you two so we can go fuck like sex crazed nymphs. I did not say that out loud. Roni was faster with a response.

"Dad, I've been talking with Dirk about showing him some sights over the weekend."

"Ah, good. Mike and I will likely be chatting about boring family stories. You two should go and have some fun. Let's have a drink and play some darts first."

We entered the very old pub, and I looked around. The place was full, with groups of British men and a few women huddled around small tables, sipping on their pints of beer. I did not know what to order, so I tried a mild lager, while Fred and Mike got a stout ale, and Roni got a lager and lime. I tasted hers and liked it better. She laughed.

"That's a lady's drink, mate! But nobody will think worse of you, they know you're a Yank."

Fred and Mike stepped up to the dart board and started playing with a couple of locals. Roni sat close to me and ran her hand up my thigh under the table. She gazed into my eyes from six inches away.

"God, I want you! How in the world did you do this to me? I'm very close to clearing the table and having you mount me here in front of my friends and neighbors!"

I laughed as I slid my hand up her thigh under the cover of the table.

"Every now and then a woman and I have this sort of attraction to each other. It's just hormones and sexual chemistry."

She leaned over and kissed my ear, sticking her tongue in it. It felt very nice. My cock stirred and I felt a tingle all the way to my toes.

"And what do you do in these circumstances, Mister Caldwell?"

The strong English beer was working on me already.

"Well, Miss Veronica. I get the woman alone and we satisfy the urge. Frontwards, backwards, sideways and upside down. Me on top, you on top, lots of fucking and sucking. How's that sound?"

She shuddered and squeezed my thigh.

"Good lord, man! I think my panties are getting wet with all this talk! I'm incredibly randy! We need to do it, now!"

"While a great notion, it's impractical at present."

She looked around the pub and then got a sly smile on her face.

"I have a very naughty idea, Dirk."

I was all ears.

"What's that, Roni?"

She grinned and blushed.

"Let's go to the loo together and have a quickie!"

The loo being the restroom did not seem like a romantic location for an introductory tryst.

"That would be a first for me. Won't people notice?"

She shook her head.

"The loo is in the back, off a dim hallway. Give me a minute or two head start, then come knock on the door of the ladies room. I'll let you in and we'll have a quick shag."

She rose and headed for the rear of the pub. I snuck a look at my watch just as Fred and Mike came back to the table. Fred looked around for his daughter.

"Where's Roni?"

I inclined my head to the rear of the pub.

"Gone to the loo."

I thought it best not to say that I would be following her in a minute to fuck her.

Fred nodded.

"We ordered another round, we're next up for billiards now."

I arose.

"That strong lager! I'm off to the loo in that case."

Fred and Mike laughed and engaged in more conversation as I headed to the back.

I found the ladies room in the dim hallway and furtively tapped on the door. Roni peeked out, looked around to see if there were any witnesses, then pulled me in and shut the door. She took my face in both hands and started kissing me passionately. My male member started rising to the occasion as we kissed.

She stepped back breathlessly and looked at me.

"Well, now."

I lifted her off her feet and perched her ass on the sink, as her legs went around me as she giggled. I lifted her mini skirt and found the top of her leggings and pulled them down to her ankles along with her damp panties. In turn, she unfastened my slacks, and they dropped to my ankles as she pulled my fully erect cock out of my underwear.

"Oh, God! It's perfect! So hard ..."

I stepped closer to her and pushed the engorged purple head of my cock against her wet labia and rubbed the head up and down her slit a few times as she groaned. Looking down at her lovely thick pubic hair, I decided she was a natural redhead. I started working the head of my cock into her pussy as our eyes met. I smiled at her.

"Ready?"

She smiled and nodded her head.

As I started to push in, she grabbed my dick with a hand and called out, "Wait!"

I stopped my thrust just in time; besides she had a handful of cock that wasn't going anywhere. She had a good grip.

"Dirk, I just remembered! I don't have my birth control in! You mustn't ejaculate in me! I'm probably ready to ovulate."

The way she said ejaculate was cool. Like 'Eee zhock you late.'

"Okay, got it. A dry contact."

She looked puzzled. It was an Air Force tanker crew term, an inside joke.

"I mean, I won't come in you."

She looked serious.

"Promise?"

I nodded.

"I promise."

She grinned.

"Well, then flyboy. Give me a little taste of what you've got!"

She removed her hand, and I answered by pushing straight in. She gasped and her eyes rolled back in her head as she held my arms. I lifted her legs up and drilled in deep. She felt fantastic, so hot and wet.

"Oh, God! Oh, God! It's all I had hoped for! Oh, my!"

I stroked her pretty good as she rocked on the sink, moaning, then sticking a knuckle in her mouth to stifle her noises. It was very sexy, and after only a few minutes I could feel the urge to cum building rapidly.

"Roni, I'm so hot I'm about to come! I'm pulling out!"

True to my word, I pulled out and she exclaimed as she took my slimy cock in her hand and started stroking it hard.

"I'll finish you off with a quick rub of your willy!"

She no sooner said that when my cock erupted, squirting sticky cum up past her head, getting a spatter on her glasses, her cheek, some in her hair, and the rest on the wall. Roni squealed as she turned her head away from the torrent of man juice that was decorating her in various places.

After a moment of surprise, she laughed.

"Well, that proves you did not spray your seed in me, because it's all over me!"

I was contrite.

"Sorry, Roni!"

She laughed again and shook her head.

"Wipe off and go back to the table, I'll be along as soon as I get rid of the evidence."

I wiped my dripping dick off with some toilet paper and snuck out of the loo just in time, as a lady approached just as I was leaving. At least she was not outside the door when I came out.

Sitting down at the table, I gratefully took a drink of beer and looked around for Fred and Mike. They were engrossed in a game of billiards across the room and did not see me right away. Mike came back to the table a moment later and took a drink of his beer. He looked at me.

"Having fun, Dirk?"

I smiled at him. If he only knew.

"Yeah, it's great. This is better than hanging out on the base."

He nodded knowingly.

"It sure is. I love hanging out with Uncle Fred. And Veronica, she's nice, don't you think?"

I smiled again.

"She's a peach. Lots of fun, and very cute, too."

He nodded again.

"You should ask her out, go see some sights."

"So that's okay with you? How about Fred?"

He grinned.

"He'll be fine with it. That way he feels like she is being entertained while he and I visit."

Mike went back to the billiards table about the time Roni got back to the table. Her face and hair looked good; you couldn't tell that only a few minutes ago I had shot cum all over her.

She sat down and turned toward me with a grin.

"Well! That was bloody great fun!"

I had to laugh at her excitement.

She went on, "I loved that quick shag, but it only whetted my appetite for more. Say you'll be a dear and come by my flat and give me a proper session!"

I squeezed her thigh under the table.

"A gentleman always keeps working until the lady is satisfied."

She smiled and held my hand under the table.

"This lady plans on being very satisfied. Now, we must escape this venue and go to my flat."

We sipped our beers and chatted for a while, comparing histories. Fred and Mike came back to the table after their game, talking animatedly. After a few minutes, Fred looked around for the waitress.

"Let's have one more!"

Roni took the opportunity to escape.

"Dad, Dirk and I are going to walk back to my flat and listen to some music and talk where it's not so noisy. It's near his bus stop anyway."

Both Fred and Mike nodded approvingly.

"That sounds fine. I'm glad Dirk can walk you back. Hope to see you again while you are here, Dirk."

I smiled as we stood to leave.

"I certainly hope so. See you, Mike. Good night, Fred."

We exited the pub into the cool evening air. Roni held my arm close to her as we walked. I looked at her after a minute.

"So, we're going to listen to music?"

She laughed.

"I'll have to put something on so the neighbors won't hear me screaming."

I grinned.

"That's more like it."

Veronica got her desire and was satisfied with a proper session that night and several more during my trip to England. We traded letters for a while, then that tapered off and stopped. We never saw each other again on my many subsequent trips to England.

Jeri

I was in Destin, Florida on an Air Force trip from our base in Louisiana to Eglin AFB, FL. I was 36 years old and an Air Force Master Sergeant at the time of this encounter.

The situation was critical. I was within seconds of violating several sections of the Uniform Code of Military Justice (UCMJ), mainly the sections on sodomy and adultery. Article 125 of the UCMJ defines sodomy as "unnatural carnal copulation" with another person of the same sex, another person of the opposite sex, or an animal. The UCMJ is quite specific, and the article specifically says that the slightest oral or anal penetration is considered copulation. In this instance, I was about to engage in deep oral copulation with a member of the opposite sex.

Sergeant Jeri (Not her real name), whom I outranked and who was technically a subordinate was about to take my penis in her mouth and thus we were about to violate Article 125. The adultery article would be violated soon after, if things went as I hoped. To ensure that we were having consensual relations, I tried to assure myself we were legal in that respect.

As she was about to take my cock in her mouth, I asked, "Are you sure you are okay with this?"

She looked up at me and smiled.

"Sure! I want to suck your dick before we fuck!"

Well, okay then. Jeri was cleared in hot as we Air Force guys say sometimes. She had consented to sex and as far as the UCMJ was concerned, oral copulation.

I came to be in this precarious position by several events. A mission had been set up for me to evaluate a piece of cargo that the A-10 folks at Eglin had decided due to its unusual configuration needed special certification by a headquarters level guy - me - to be included in our special cargo section. Along with that, a cargo training mission had been arranged for the local air freight troops to do a practice load on our airplane. I was assigned to the Eighth Air Force HQ and would certify the outsize cargo piece. Then I would act as an instructor for the aircrew to coach them through the cargo load.

Assigned to the mission were two enlisted members of my aircrew specialty, along with the Chief of the squadron. It was Florida in February, after all. Other members of the crew were two pilots and two flight engineers. We arrived at midday on a Tuesday, with the load test and cargo training on Wednesday. We would depart late Thursday afternoon for some night training on the way home.

On arrival, I coordinated the next day's activity, and we headed for the Ft Walton Beach, FL strip after stopping by the base billeting office. Our hotel was a second-rate facility just off highway 98 and Santa Rosa Avenue, but it had a great swimming pool just off the inland waterway. The entire crew changed to swim gear and met at the pool fortified by supplies we had obtained from a local liquor store. Sergeant Jeri was the only female on the crew, and everyone paid attention to her.

Jeri was in her early 30s, and had a plump, short figure, with dyed blonde hair, and a cheery disposition. I had flown with her once when I was a squadron evaluator and had to downgrade her based on her performance. She seemed to hold no ill will toward me for that event. After looking at her in her bathing suit sitting around the pool, I was not excited by her and considered her just another face in a flight suit. We ended up sitting beside each other at dinner and I felt no special spark.

The next day, I conducted the evaluation of the special cargo in minutes and then got on with the cargo training for the crew. It was productive, and we finished early. Our next duty was a late afternoon show time for the flight home the next day, so we headed back to the hotel to change into swim gear and headed for the beach to enjoy the late afternoon and get into party mode. Sometime during the afternoon, I looked at Jeri closely as she chattered away on the beach wearing her one-piece bathing suit and decided I wanted to fuck her, just for the hell of it. Now, how to accomplish that goal?

Most women in the military had a lot of men trying to fuck them, so I would have to separate myself from the admiring crowd. I decided to be charming at dinner and drinks after and see where that led.

Most of the crew went to dinner, and I had dressed for a date with a nice button up short sleeved shirt, dark slacks, and shiny penny loafers. Jeri had a pretty floral blouse, white slacks, and sandals. Most of the other crew wore tee shirts and jeans. At dinner, Jeri was outgoing and friendly, and some of the crew went with us to a bar afterwards. I danced with her a few times, with her smiling and chatting as we did so.

Time moved on, and a smaller crew went to another bar, and we had several drinks and danced again. Jeri was smiley and friendly, and with more drinks in her, she danced closer and more intimately. We were not there yet, but progress was being made.

We went to a third bar with only my flight engineers and Jeri. Neither of the engineers were interested in dancing with Jeri, so I handled that duty. With more drinks in her, Jeri danced even more closely with her arms around my neck while she smiled at me adoringly and moved her pelvis against mine. Things were looking good.

As the evening wore on, we chatted more intimately and danced even closer. Near closing time, she smiled at me and reached for my cock and stroked it while we danced. I had a medium boner from all the pelvic contact, and her stroking felt good. I was hoping the engineers had not noticed the attention I was getting. I decided to change venues at that point, and gathered up Jeri, said goodbye to my engineers, who were lost in a technical discussion about something.

We scurried across highway 98 without getting killed and held hands on the way to the hotel. We went to my room, and on entering, we embraced and kissed for the first time. Our hands roamed each other's bodies outside our clothing. Things were looking up. She excused herself to the bathroom, and I thought it odd that she ran water so I could not hear her urinate.

Both of us were pretty tipsy, and as we reengaged, smiled at each other. Then she decided to remove my shirt by pulling it apart, stripping off the buttons while grinning. Shit, that was one of my favorite shirts.

I took a more conservative approach to getting her blouse off, using the buttons as they were intended. Soon her blouse was off, and I reached around and unfastened her bra. Her small breasts were in view, and I caressed them and kissed the nipples as she sighed and moaned a little. I noted that her breasts were about the size of teacups.

In return, Jeri reached for my slacks, unfastened them and they dropped to my ankles. She slid my underwear down, stroked my erect cock, then went to her knees and prepared to take my cock in her mouth. That's when I asked if she was okay with this. With that exchange taken care of, she commenced an enthusiastic and sloppy blow job.

After a bit, she rose up with saliva dripping from her lips, and I sat down on the edge of one of the beds and pulled her to me. I unfastened her nice slacks and slid them and her panties over her hips and down her legs where she kicked them off, then she straddled me with her exposed pussy rubbing against my hard cock.

We kissed again, and she ran her hands over my bare chest and then reached for my cock again and stroked it some more. With a smile on her face, she rose up and looked into my eyes and guided my dick between her labia and into the vaginal vault as she sat down on it with a gasp of pleasure. Her pussy was smooth, pleasantly snug, wet and slippery. Fantastic. I had achieved my short-term goal. I was fucking Sergeant Jeri.

We fucked like that for a few minutes, kissing passionately as she rocked her hips back and forth as I drove my rock-hard dick up into her. It felt great. Then she conveyed that she wanted to change positions.

She panted, "Let me get on my back so you can fuck me hard! I like It hard!"

After rising from my cock, she rolled onto the bed to her back and guided my red hot meat missile to her labia as I knelt between her legs.

I was pretty horny, so I split the lips and slipped my cock into her wet pussy and gave her a few good strokes as she moaned deeply.

Then I pulled out and went down on her moderately hairy pussy, licking her clit and probing into her vaginal vault with my tongue, searching for her G spot. I made contact with that sensitive spot and was rewarded with deep groans and exclamations.

"Oh! Yes! Oh, yeah! That's it! Oh, shit! Oh, God! Get back on me! Fuck me! Fuck me now!"

I rose up and slipped my rock hard meat back into Jeri as she moaned and groaned heavily. I stroked her hard as I raised her legs up and drilled her deep and with gusto. That was what she wanted.

"OH! YEAH! HARDER! COME ON! OH, YEAH! HOLY SHIT! OH, THAT FEELS GOOD!"

I kept up the pace and intensity and was rewarded with a low howl as she came.

"OOHHHH! YEAH! AWW SHIT!"

I felt her pussy spasm around my dick as she came, and while her body shuddered, I caressed her small breasts and tweaked her nipples. I waited patiently, although I still had a hard dick that needed to be emptied. I kept up a smooth stroking as she regained her senses. She came around with a grin and wanted more.

"Oh, man! That was intense! Let me up for a minute, will you?"

"Sure."

I got off her and my slimy erect dick bobbed as she hopped up and went to my dresser where she had spotted a bottle of Jim Beam bourbon I had bought earlier. She grabbed the bottle and took a big drink from the neck of the bottle as I looked on. I had a question.

"Does that mix with what you were drinking?"

She had a mad grin.

"I was drinking rum and coke, so I hope this mixes!"

I shrugged, pretty sure that would not mix well. She gulped down another swallow and was ready to proceed, flopping back down on her back.

"I'm ready! Let's drain that cock!"

I pushed my cock back into her as she sighed with pleasure.

"Ah, that's it! Yeah!"

I started a hard stroking and was feeling good. I kept it up and listened as Jeri exclaimed.

"Oh! Wow! Come on and bang me hard! Yeah!"

I love vocal women during sex. It leaves no doubt about how things are going. Now, I wanted to do her from behind.

"Let's roll over, Jeri. I want to do you doggie style!"

"Oh, yeah! For sure!"

I pulled out and she rolled onto her elbows and knees. I slid my cock back into her from behind and started stroking her hard, watching her plump ass jiggle as I plowed her while admiring her tan lines. She was still vocal.

"Yeah! Give it to me hard! Oh, wow! Yeah!"

I ramped up the rate and intensity and was soon pounding her as hard as I ever had.

"Yeah! Oh, yeah! C'mon! Fuck me hard!"

Within a few minutes I felt the urge building and shot a load of hot cum deep into Jeri. I let out a loud moan.

"Oh, yeah! Thanks, Jeri! That felt great!"

I pulled out, and she rolled onto her back and relaxed back into the bed, grinning up at me.

"That was cool! Where in the world did you learn to eat pussy like that?"

"I took lessons from an Italian sexpot."

"You were paying attention. I've never come so hard! Damn, that was good!"

Then she shook her head and yawned.

"Man, I'm sleepy. That bourbon did a number on me. Let's take a nap and do it again!"

"Sounds good to me."

We lay against each other, and soon fell asleep.

After a few hours of sleep, I awoke with a start. I was feeling warm and wet down at my midsection. Then I realized that Jeri had pissed on us. I woke her by pushing on her shoulder.

"Jeri! Wake up! You're pissing the bed!"

She shook her head as she woke up.

"Oh, shit! I was sleeping so hard! Did I piss on the bed?"

We were laying in a wet bed, so yeah.

"Let's get up, Jeri. We're all wet!"

We both climbed out of bed and I saw that we were covered in Jeri pee, as well as the bed.

"Head to the bathroom, Jeri. let's get cleaned up."

We staggered into the bathroom, and I put her on the toilet as she held her head in her hands.

"Man, I'm so wasted. I'm so sorry I pissed in the bed!"

"While you're there, go ahead and empty your bladder."

"Yeah, good idea. Can you step outside the door for a minute?"

"Sure."

I did and after a minute she called out.

"All done."

I stood her up and ran some warm water, then soaped up a washcloth and started wiping her down as she held onto my shoulders. After washing her legs and belly as well as I could, I washed myself off. She then had a comment.

"Man, check you out! You've sprung a boner."

She reached out to my cock and stroked it, with a big grin on her face.

"You got turned on wiping me down, how sweet."

"I had no idea cleaning pee off a woman could be so erotic."

She laughed.

"I think you're just a horny little fucker. Go ahead and do me again before we go back to bed."

I had to shake my head, but her stroking felt pretty good.

"Are you sure? You're pretty wasted."

She nodded.

"I'm okay, I know what I'm doing. Do me right here, right now!"

"In the bathroom? Okay."

I picked her up and sat her ass on the edge of the bathroom counter. She squealed and laughed at that, and spread her legs wide, guiding me to her pussy. I pushed in with little resistance and started pumping into her.

"This is a new thing for me. I was thinking you were going to bend me over the toilet!"

"That would not be gentlemanly."

She laughed.

"It wouldn't be my first time that happened."

Jeri wrapped her arms around my neck and closed her eyes as I fucked her. She was smiling and was very relaxed, not moving. For a while I thought she may have passed out, but occasionally she would moan and move her hands, stroking my hair and holding onto my ass. It really was erotic. I could feel pressure building in my balls.

"Oh, Jeri! I'm about to come!"

She opened her eyes and looked into mine.

"Yeah! Do it! Come in me!"

I let loose a torrent of hot cum into her already slick pussy. After groaning in pleasure and enjoying the last spasm of semen, I opened my eyes and saw her looking at me with a smile.

"Well, now. That was different. Let me wipe off and we'll try sleeping again."

I went back to the other bed and pulled the covers back. We both climbed in and snuggled a little, falling asleep quickly. I hoped we would make it until a reasonable wake up time. It was not to be.

After not very long, perhaps an hour or two, I was again rudely awakened. I heard Jeri groaning loudly. My eyes opened and I looked at Jeri. She was sound asleep, groaning as if she was in pain. I shook her by the shoulder.

"Jeri! Are you alright?"

She came awake with a start.

"What's wrong? What time is it?"

"You were groaning. Are you sick?"

She shook her head sleepily.

"No, I just do that sometimes. It's probably because I was so wasted when we went back to bed. I can sense a hangover on the way, though. I think I'm still a little drunk. What time did you say it was?"

I looked at my watch in the dark.

"0430." (4:30 am for you civilians)

She yawned and stretched.

"Oh, shit! That's too early to get up. What do you want to do now?"

"Like what do you mean? I wouldn't mind getting some more sleep."

She curled up against me.

"Yeah, that would be great. What shall we do to get sleepy again?"

A small hand had found its way to my cock, which started stirring immediately as she started stroking it.

I said, "That feels great, but are you up for it?"

She grinned.

"Yeah, come on when you are ready. You can kiss my boobs if you want."

I leaned over and kissed the little boobs and nibbled the nipples as Jeri continued to stroke my rapidly awakening cock. She smiled sleepily.

"Go ahead, Dirk. I'm really sleepy, so just get on me and get going."

"Okay, just checking that you are okay with this."

"Yeah, yeah. Just get on me and give me a good night fuck."

I moved between her legs and entered her slippery hole.

She sighed and moaned.

"Yeah, that's good. Go ahead and do it nice and slow. I might doze off, just keep going."

I shrugged and started stroking her slowly. It felt good to me, and Jeri was laying back smiling with her eyes closed as she pulled her knees up to get me deeper, so I kept going.

"Mmm. Yeah, Dirk. That will put us to sleep. Go ahead and come when you want."

"You got it."

I stroked her smoothly and slowly, enjoying the ride. She moved her legs down next to mine and hooked her ankles over mine. Every now and then I leaned down to kiss her boobies and sometimes she would moan a little. She was very quiet, occasionally stroking my hair with one hand, while the other rested on my ass.

"Mmm. I like holding your ass while you push into me."

"And I like you holding my ass. It feels nice."

Several quiet minutes later, she started stirring and making quiet sounds of pleasure.

"Mmm. Mmm. Ahh. Mmm."

Her hips, which had been motionless to this point, started moving into me a little. She stiffened a little, then the hand on my ass moved, and one of her fingers started exploring my anus, which was interesting. She then made a few more sounds, then relaxed.

"Ahh, that was nice. A sweet little mini-orgasm. Thank you, sir."

I grinned.

"You don't have to call me sir in bed, Sergeant."

She giggled sleepily and squeezed my ass cheek, having removed her finger from my asshole.

"So noted, Master Sergeant."

I kept up the gentle fuck for a few more minutes. I felt the urge building, and then shot a load of cum into Jeri as she lay with her eyes closed. I was pretty sure she had passed out or fallen asleep, but then she wrapped her legs around my back and pushed her hips into me as she groaned.

"Mmm. That was nice. Goodnight."

We awoke a few hours later without any further drama and she dressed quickly and headed for her room, agreeing to meet for breakfast at the hotel restaurant in a half hour or so. We were the only ones from our crew in the place and were able to speak candidly about our night together.

She began.

"That was kind of an unexpected turn of events last night. I thought you just liked to dance, then I felt a boner that wouldn't go away."

I smiled.

"Sometime on the beach yesterday, I got the urge to sleep with you."

She laughed.

"Aw, c'mon, Dirk. I don't have a great beach body. Thanks, though. Sometime while we were dancing, I started getting horny for you."

"Thanks for letting me know. That was a very effective method of communicating your desire to get laid."

That got a hard laugh out of her, and she covered her mouth and blushed. When she got herself under control, she responded.

"Nothing like grabbing a man's dick to get his attention!"

"Like I said, very effective."

Then she looked concerned.

"Sorry about wetting your bed. Will the hotel charge you for that?"

I shrugged.

"I don't know. I'll let them know when I check out."

She shook her head.

"Damn, I was wasted. It was fun, though. How many times did you come?"

"Umm, three times. Twice in the bed and once in the bathroom."

That got her laughing hard again.

"I can't believe we did that!"

"Yeah, it was kind of spontaneous. A first for me."

She laughed again, then got a quiet look.

"Well, we had a fun night, and I enjoyed doing it with you a lot."

She emphasized this with a smile.

"I liked it a lot! But we probably should not continue this."

I nodded.

"I agree. I violated several articles of the UCMJ, and I don't want to put you in a spot."

"Yeah. Well, thanks for a memorable night. It was really satisfying."

She reached for my hand and squeezed it across the table smiling at me. She released my hand just in time, as some members of our crew showed up.

"Hey! Mind if we join you guys?"

Jeri and I looked up and smiled.

"Sure, pull up a chair."

One of the pilots looked at us as he sat down, then teased us.

"Say, you guys having breakfast together so early. What have you been up to?"

Jeri didn't skip a beat.

"Well, Sergeant Caldwell and I drank and danced until closing time, then came back to the hotel and had great sex until dawn, showered together, and came here to eat."

They looked at us and laughed.

"Yeah, sure. What are you guys having? It looks good!"

Jeri and I looked at each other and smiled. I was thinking a shower together would have been nice.

We flew back to our base, parted ways, and I thought that was that.

A week or so later, she called me at my office. After greeting each other, she had an unexpected announcement.

"Dirk, I'm going crazy wanting more head from you!"

I looked around my office at my colleagues on the phone or diligently working on paperwork and tried to keep a straight face while my loins stirred.

"That sounds serious. What did you have in mind?"

"Let's do lunch, then go to your place and do it all afternoon."

"That sounds like a helluva lot more fun than office work! I suppose I can take a long lunch."

I made my excuses and left the office to meet Jeri at the agreed upon time. She was waiting for me at the headquarters building security checkpoint, and we walked to her car, then headed for an upscale bar and grill off base. After a cheerful lunch, she couldn't stand it anymore. Reaching for my crotch under the table, she squeezed my dick through my uniform pants. I had to laugh.

"I did not wake up this morning expecting that!"

She giggled.

"I can't help it! I'm horny for you! Let's go to your place."

We drove to my nearby apartment, and upon entering, she gave me a tight embrace and started a passionate kiss. Our hands wandered each other's body outside our clothes, with our libido rising quickly. She pulled back and breathlessly made a request.

"Let's get naked and get to it!"

"Okay, but I'm taking my own clothes off! You trashed one of my favorite shirts last time we did this!"

That got a good laugh from her.

"Okay, you can undress yourself, but I want you to take mine off."

"Deal!"

I carefully took off my uniform and neatly hung it. Soon I was in my underwear.

"Your turn!"

As she smiled and softly moaned, I caressed her as I slowly unbuttoned her clothes and slowly and sensually removed them. Soon she was in only her panties. I kissed her boobs and nibbled the nipples as I ran my hands over her. Standing still, she let me kiss her up and down her entire body. She was impatient.

"Come on, Dirk. Let's get on the bed!"

"Not yet, baby. I'm wanting to get you worked up first."

She pulled my head to her and kissed me hard.

"I'm fucking worked up enough!"

We were still in the living room, so I turned on some music and pulled Jeri to me.

"Let's dance."

She shook her head in exasperation and then put her arms around my neck as we started to dance in our underwear. Within seconds, she was stroking my boner through my underpants and grinning at me.

"That's more fun than down in Florida."

"It is. We would have had more fun dancing in our underwear in front of the flight engineers."

That got a laugh from her, and she moved closer to me as we swayed with the music.

"Damn, this is fun."

I stroked her ass inside her panties as we danced.

"Yes, it is. It sets a certain mood. Ready to go to the bed?"

She almost trotted to the bedroom.

"Yes!"

Jeri lay on the bed, then I bent down to pull her underwear off with my teeth.

"Oh, shit. That's sexy."

"Yeah. Now your turn."

She pulled her underwear off with her teeth, needing a hand to get it over my boner. She gave my cock a kiss as she went by.

"Mmm. Nice touch!"

I kissed her legs from her crotch to her toes, sucking on the toes for a minute. I thought she would come right then and there.

"Oh! Shit! That is awesome!"

I went to her pussy and sucked her clit with my tongue shaped like a straw. Jeri writhed in a wave of pleasure. I stuck my tongue in her vaginal vault and tickled her G spot with my tongue. She moaned and squirmed with pleasure.

"OH! SHIT! THAT IS SO FUCKING GOOD! THAT'S WHAT I WANTED! OH, YEAH!"

Keeping up the attack on her G spot and clit, I started to caress her boobies, squeezing the nipples as I did so.

"AH! OH! AH, SHIT! OH, DAMN! AHHHHH! YES! YES! OH! AAAHHHHH!!"

Jeri came almost immediately with a loud scream of ecstasy as I continued my attention to her most sensitive areas. She had been pretty worked up.

As she shuddered with delight while the wave of orgasm washed over her, I moved between her legs and got my cock into play, pushing between her wet lips and entering her pussy.

"OH! YEAH! OH, FUCK ME, DIRK!"

I stroked her steadily for a few minutes until she regained her senses, then as she grinned at me, I had a suggestion.

"Let's put you on top. I want you to ride me."

She laughed.

"Oh, yeah! That will be great! I'm still tingling!"

I pulled out and rolled onto my back. She swung aboard and guided my meat missile into her and settled down onto my cock.

"Oh! That's deep! Yeah!"

She started moving her hips back and forth, but she could be doing much better.

"Jeri, push your hips toward me like you are using your clit to erase my pubic hair. Really push it down and forward."

"Okay! Oh, wow! That is so great! OH SHIT!"

I had to smile. She would be coming again, and soon.

"OH! AH! OOHH! OH, SHIT! DAMN! AAAHHHH!"

In a couple of minutes, Jeri came again, the second time within five minutes. I kept up a steady thrusting into her, enjoying the feel of her pussy spasming around my rock hard cock.

"AHHHH! OHHH! SHIT, DIRK! I'M COMING AGAIN!"

Another howl of pleasure escaped her lips, and she collapsed onto me as I continued to stroke into her. Jeri gasped out her satisfaction.

"Oh fuck, Dirk! That's amazing! Twice in one fuck! Wow!"

"Let me roll you over, I want to do you from on top."

"Yeah, that would be nice. I'm fucking tingling all over!"

I managed to get us rolled over, and after a few strokes felt like I was going to come, so I pulled out to cool off. I wasn't ready yet. I rolled off to the side and spreading her legs, put my finger in her pussy and started working over her G spot.

"OH! Shit, Dirk! That's on fire! Oh, man!"

I eased up on the pressure and enjoyed watching her writhe on the bed, babbling.

"Man, oh man! That's some feeling! Oh, my! Oh!"

Then I ramped up the action by leaning down to suck her clit while I fingered her. She was going crazy.

"Ahhh! Oh, damn! Oh! It's like it's on fire and won't stop! Oh, Dirk! Get on me and fuck me hard! Please!"

I knelt between her legs.

"Suck me!"

She sat up and took my cock in her mouth and started giving me a very enthusiastic blow job. After a minute, she pulled back.

"Come on, Dirk! Fuck me now! Please! I'm on fire!"

I eased up and pushed into her, getting a groan of pleasure. She raised her knees to her chest as I started a fast, hard rhythm.

"Yeah! Oh, yeah! Do it harder!"

With that encouragement, I took her ankles and raised them up and rested them on my shoulders. Her ass was raised off the sheets, and her dripping wet pussy was unprotected. It was time to finish the job.

I started fucking her hard, the sound of slapping flesh filling the room as her sopping wet pussy took my assault. I reached down and squeezed her tits as I pounded away. I was doing her so hard her cheeks were jiggling every time my pelvis rammed into her. She had ahold of my ass cheeks with both hands, as if trying to pull me deeper.

"OH GOD! OH! YES! YES! YES! OH, SHIT! AAHHHHH!! OH, SWEET JESUS! OH!"

She came while screaming, loudly and long, as if her heart were being torn from her chest. She pushed back into me as hard as she could, as I drilled her deeply, trying to push her through the bed. I came with a pent up load of cum, filling her pussy with spurt after long spurt of sticky semen. I also howled out my satisfaction.

After a moment, her orgasm subsided, and I felt her collapse back into the bed. I thought she had passed out. I lowered her legs and reached for her face. Her eyes were closed, and she was panting heavily. Patting her face, I asked how she was doing.

Her eyes opened and took a while to focus, as if she was disoriented. After a moment, a shy smile appeared, and she took my hand while looking into my eyes.

"Now I understand what swooning is all about. Damn, I felt like I was unconscious for a minute. I'm good now. Tired, happy, and very fucking satisfied. Damn! Three hard orgasms in one fuck. Holy shit! How do you do that?"

I smiled at her.

"I had lessons."

"No shit. Damn, I've never been fucked so hard or had such a hard orgasm in my life! Incredible! I hope I can walk out of here unassisted."

She reached up and pulled my head down and started showering me with kisses.

"Thank you, thank you, thank you! I'm going to treasure that memory for some time."

I pulled back and withdrew my sopping wet limp dick from her and raised up.

"We'd better get cleaned up. I should be getting back to work."

We went to the bathroom and got a wet cloth and started wiping each other down. I really needed a shower but did not have time. After dressing, we met in the living room and shared one last kiss.

She looked into my eyes from a few inches away.

"Well, Sergeant Caldwell, thanks for lunch. I'm sure we will see each other around the base. We should probably not ... date ... anymore. I'm afraid we'll get caught, and you are on your way to the top, I just know it."

"Thanks, Jeri. That makes sense. I've enjoyed our date."

She grinned.

"I REALLY enjoyed it!"

She drove me back to the headquarters building, then reached for my hand before I got out.

"Thanks again for a wonderful experience, Dirk. I don't think I'll be able to top it! You've made me feel incredible! When we see each other in the squadron or around base, if our eyes meet, you'll know I'll be thinking of coming three times this afternoon, and our crazy night in Ft. Walton Beach."

I squeezed her hand.

"Me too, Jeri. Thanks!"

I got out and walked up the long sidewalk to the entryway. I turned around as I reached for the door. She was still looking at me. We gazed at each other for a moment, then I turned away and entered the building. It was over.

We saw each other in passing at the squadron a few times in the months ahead and said hello but played it cool, but we did trade private looks and a smile, remembering. Eventually she moved to a different base, and many years later I saw her at a military reunion. We nodded and smiled at each other but did not speak, but I'm sure were thinking of the same thing.

Don't miss out!

Visit the website below and you can sign up to receive emails whenever Dirk Caldwell publishes a new book. There's no charge and no obligation.

https://books2read.com/r/B-A-UHDZ-ASCEF

Did you love *To All the Girls I've Loved Before: Sexy Short Stories Book 3*? Then you should read *A Layover in Omaha with Tina*[1] by Dirk Caldwell!

Dirk's novels are written from the male perspective, but both men and women will enjoy them.

Airline pilot Dirk has an unexpected layover in Omaha and meets Tina on a double date. Although she is 65 years old, her sexy attitude and chemistry with Dirk draw them together for an extended evening of passion and discovery. Enjoy the exquisite details as the author weaves the story into a compelling description of their night so intensely, that the reader will feel they are in the bedroom with the couple. You won't be able to put this book down!

---

1. https://books2read.com/u/bre5JZ

2. https://books2read.com/u/bre5JZ

Also by Dirk Caldwell

Adventures of Stan
Stan does a Big Girl and gives her a Big Orgasm
Stan Does a Female Police Officer While On Duty
Stan Scores on a Booty Call with Barbara
Stan Takes Barb's Anal Cherry
Stan Teaches Oklahoma Karen About Sex in the City
Stan gets Kinky with Barb on Vacation
Barb Wants more Orgasms with Stan before She gets Engaged to
Another Man
Stan Does Barbara's Mom!
Stan Titty Fucks Barbara's Friend!

Dirk Caldwell Romantic Erotic Novels
A Visit to the Farm with Darla - a Sexy Short Story
A Layover in Omaha with Tina
A Night in Eufaula with Lynn
A Trip to the Lake with Kim
Older Women need Love, too! Erika visits Atlanta
Lessons in Love: Gabriella visits Indianapolis
Big Girls Need Love, too! Barbara from Kokomo
Flight Attendants want Love: Flying High with Jessica
Back to the Farm with Darla - A Sexy Sequel

Redheads need Love: Megan from New Orleans
A Big Girl finds Love: Joann from Shreveport
Lust from London: My Affair with a British Nymphomaniac
Paula's Sexy European Weekend
Mother and Daughter Threesome

Dirk Caldwell Sexy Short Stories
To All the Girls I've Loved Before: Sexy Short Stories Book 1
To All the Girls I've Loved Before: Sexy Short Stories Book 2
To All the Girls I've Loved Before: Sexy Short Stories Book 3

About the Author

Dirk Caldwell is the pen name of the author of an erotic book series. Dirk embodies the life experiences of the author as an Air Force veteran and commercial airline pilot. Most of the content is true and relates to the author's experiences. It's up to the reader to decide what is fiction and what is true life.